The Elves and the Shoemaker

A retelling by Violet Findley • Illustrated by Martha Aviles

Once upon a time, there lived a kind
shoemaker and his wife. Times were hard
and they became very, very poor.

One day, they had only enough leather
to make a single pair of shoes.

The shoemaker put the leather on his table. "Tomorrow, I will make one last pair of shoes to sell at the market," he said sadly.

But a magical thing happened. When the
shoemaker woke up, the leather had already
been turned into a fancy pair of shoes!
"Wow! I will sell these at the market," he said.

The shoemaker sold the shoes for a bag of
gold. With the gold, he bought more leather.

The shoemaker put the leather on his table.
The next morning, he found two fancy
pairs of shoes!
"Wow! I will sell these at the market," he said.
And so he did.

Again, the shoemaker used the gold to buy more leather. He put the leather on the table. The next morning, he found three fancy pairs of shoes!

Life went on like this for many months.
In time, the shoemaker and his wife sold
many shoes and became very, very rich.

The shoemaker and his wife were happy, but also very curious. Who was making all the fancy shoes? One night, they decided to find out. Instead of going to bed, they hid behind a curtain.

When the clock struck midnight, in came
two little elves. Zippity, zip! They made 100
pairs of the fanciest shoes ever seen. Then
they danced a joyful jig and left.

"Two elves have been making the shoes!"
said the shoemaker.
"Did you see their tattered clothes? Let's
make them some new ones to say thank
you," said his wife.

All day, the shoemaker and his wife worked and worked. She made two tiny outfits. He made two tiny pairs of shoes.

They put the new clothes on the table and
hid. When the clock struck midnight, in
came the two elves.

The elves were surprised to see the fine
clothes instead of the leather. Zippity, zip!
They put on the shirts, pants, and shoes.
Then they danced a joyful jig and left.

The shoemaker and his wife never saw
the two elves again. But thanks to their
good deeds, all four of them lived
happily ever after.